Fairy Bears

Lulu

"I promise to do my best. I promise to work hard to care for the world and all its plants, animals and children. This is the Fairy Bear Promise."

Julie Sykes lives with her family, their wolf and a flying carpet in a cottage in Hampshire. Julie first wrote about Fairy Bears after meeting Glitter the Fairy Bear in her back garden. When Julie isn't busy writing, she spends her time eating cake and having flying races with her Fairy Bear friends.

For more Fairy Bear fun visit
www.fairybearsworld.com

Look out for more magical Fairy Bears!

Dizzy

Sunny

Blossom

Sparkle

Primrose

Misty

Lulu

Poppy

Visit the secret world of the Fairy Bears and
explore the magical Crystal Caves . . .

www.fairybearsworld.com

Fairy Bears

Lulu

Julie Sykes

Illustrated by Samantha Chaffey

MACMILLAN CHILDREN'S BOOKS

First published 2011 by Macmillan Children's Books
a division of Macmillan Publishers Limited
20 New Wharf Road, London N1 9RR
Basingstoke and Oxford
Associated companies throughout the world
www.panmacmillan.com

ISBN 978-0-330-54531-0

1 3 5 7 9 8 6 4 2

A CIP catalogue record for this book is available from
the British Library.

Printed and bound in the UK by CPI Mackays, Chatham ME5 8TD

*For Samantha Swinnerton, who is
such a good friend to the Fairy Bears*

For Warren Park Primary School

FAIRY BEAR WISHES

Julie Sykes

Prologue

At the bottom of Firefly Meadow, not far
from the stream, stands a tall sycamore
tree. The tree is old with a thick grey trunk
and spreading branches. Hidden amongst
the branches is a forgotten squirrel hole. If
you could fly through the squirrel hole and
down the inside of the tree's hollow trunk,
you would find a secret door that leads to a
special place. Open the door and step inside
the magical Crystal Caves, home of the
Fairy Bears.

The Fairy Bears are always busy.
They work hard caring for nature and
children everywhere. You'll have to be
quick to see them, and you'll have to
believe in magic.

Fairy Bears

Do you believe in Fairy Bear magic? Can you keep a secret? Then come on in – the Fairy Bears would love to meet you.

Chapter One

Lulu the Fairy Bear flew into the playground just as the school bell was ringing.

"That was close," said her best friend, Poppy. "You were nearly late."

Fluttering her violet wings Lulu grinned cheekily. "I was practising air ball in Firefly Meadow."

Air ball was a fast catching game played by two teams with a ball made from a sycamore seed without its wings. Each team had eight players. The winning team was the one that scored the most goals: shooting the sycamore seed through their team's net that was magically suspended in the air. Players could fly with the ball but they weren't allowed to hold it for more than two seconds. All players could score goals. Air-ball tournaments were played in the huge air-ball stadium in the Crystal Caves, but training and friendly games mostly took place in Firefly Meadow.

Poppy was impressed.

"You must have got up very early to do that," she said.

"I did. It's the air-ball try-outs tomorrow and I'm hoping to be chosen for the school team," Lulu explained.

Poppy's mouth fell open. "But we're only juniors! You have to be a senior to be on the air-ball team."

Lulu was combing her pale gold fur

A Lesson for Lulu

into place. She stopped and looked at Poppy.

"Mrs Pan, the seniors' teacher, said I was good enough to try out," she said modestly.

"Lulu, that's fantastic!" Poppy exclaimed.

"Lulu, Poppy, stop chattering and hurry up," called their teacher, Miss Alaska.

With sheepish grins the two Fairy Bears flew across the playground and hurried to their classroom. The other Fairy Bears were already in their seats waiting.

"Good morning, everyone," said Miss Alaska, going to stand by her large stone desk. Folding her yellow-and-pink wings neatly behind her back she looked at the class. Her eyes rested on Lulu, who was fiddling with the star at the end of

5

her gold-coloured wand.

"Exciting news," said Miss Alaska. "Today Lulu is going on her first task."

Dropping her wand on the desk, Lulu sat up straight. The tasks were very important and involved helping someone, or helping the environment. She couldn't wait to get started.

"What do I have to do?" she asked eagerly.

Miss Alaska smiled. "I'm glad you're keen, but first we must say the Fairy Bear Promise," she reminded Lulu.

A Lesson for Lulu

Stone seats scraped on the floor as the Fairy Bears stood up and held paws. Lulu stood between Poppy and Misty. Closing her eyes tightly she loudly chanted the Fairy Bear Promise. Then opening her eyes she let go of Poppy and Misty, picked up her wand and waved it excitedly. The round violet topaz gemstone sparkled brightly as a flurry of stars burst from the wand's end. The stars raced each other across the classroom, dissolving as they reached the door. The class laughed and Lulu cheered.

Miss Alaska was about to hand Lulu her task, written on a large green sycamore leaf, when Mr Griz, the head Fairy Bear teacher, knocked at the class-cave door.

"Excuse me one moment," said Miss Alaska.

Impatiently Lulu waited for her teacher to finish talking to Mr Griz.

A Lesson for Lulu

"I hope I get an easy task," she whispered to Poppy.

"You'll work it out," said Poppy encouragingly.

Lulu was worried that if the task was too complicated she wouldn't be able to complete it quickly. The air-ball try-outs were early the following morning in Firefly Meadow. Lulu knew Miss Alaska would expect her to finish her task before taking part in them. But would she have time to complete her task by then? Maybe the magic mirror would know?

Lulu went and stood in front of it. At first she saw her own reflection: a sporty-looking bear with pale gold fur and pretty violet wings. Then, in a sudden swirl of violet mist, the picture disappeared. Now Lulu was staring at a girl with wavy brown hair, blue eyes, freckles and a friendly smile. The girl was trying to skip. Lulu's big brown eyes widened. Skipping was easy, so how come the girl was getting in such a tangle with the rope?

"That's it!" she exclaimed. "I'm going to teach her how to skip."

Lulu was convinced that her task was to give the girl a skipping lesson. When Miss Alaska finally handed her the

sycamore leaf she read it quickly, then read it again to make sure she'd got it right.

"I've got to help some solitary bees," she said, her face creasing with puzzlement. "What's a solitary bee?"

Primrose put her hand up. "I know," she called out. "Unlike the bumblebee, solitary bees don't live together in hives. They live alone in holes, sometimes in the ground and sometimes in the cement that holds bricks together."

"That's right. Well done, Primrose," said Miss Alaska, nodding.

"So what do I have to do?" asked Lulu.

Miss Alaska smiled mysteriously. "That's part of your task. You have to find out what the problem is before you work out how to solve it."

Lulu hid a groan. This sounded far too difficult for her liking. Why couldn't Miss

Alaska just tell her what the task was so she
could get on with it?

"Good luck, Lulu," said Miss Alaska, her
tone of voice making it clear that she would
not give her any more help.

"Thank you," said Lulu with a sigh.
She read the task through once more and
checked the map at the bottom of the leaf
that showed her where to go. It was a fair
distance but Lulu was a fast flier. Wrapping
the leaf tightly round her wand for safe
keeping, she waved goodbye to her friends
then hurried out of the classroom, heading
towards the Grand Door.

Chapter Two

The Main Tunnel was busy but Lulu
whizzed past anyone who was flying
more slowly than her. When Lulu reached
the gnarled root staircase she skipped up
the stairs two at a time. As soon as Lulu
stepped through the Grand Door, into the
hollow trunk of the sycamore, she took off
— speedily flying towards the pale circle of
light shining through the disused squirrel
hole at the top of the tree. Without stopping
Lulu flew outside into Firefly Meadow.

"Hi, Lulu," called a friendly voice.

Fairy Bears

Jet, a sporty Fairy Bear in Mrs Pan's class, waved from a branch above Lulu.

"Hi, Jet," Lulu called back.

"Are you going on a task?"

"Yes," said Lulu. "It's my first one."

"That's exciting!" Jet exclaimed. "A shame about the air-ball try-outs though."

Lulu hovered in front of Jet.

A Lesson for Lulu

"What do you mean?"

"You won't have time to do both. But you could still try out for the reserves. That's not until the day after tomorrow," said Jet encouragingly.

"But I don't want to be a reserve. They only play when someone is sick or injured and that hardly ever happens," said Lulu, her eyes glinting. "I'll *have* to finish my task today. Bye, Jet."

"Good luck," he called back as Lulu sped away. "Don't forget the tasks are very important whereas air ball is just a game."

"Just a game!" snorted Lulu. Air ball was more than that to her. Determined to complete her task in one day Lulu flew towards the house shown on her map.

Lulu treated the flight as a training exercise. Air-ball players regularly flew cross country to build up their stamina and keep fit. As she flew, Lulu concentrated on her wing stroke and breathing, but every now and then the solitary bees popped into her mind. The task had said *bees*, but if solitary bees lived on their own then why did more than one need her help? She hoped the problem wouldn't be too difficult to work out and then solve.

Lulu was delighted when she reached her destination much more quickly than she'd hoped. She hovered in the sky checking there was no one around, but the garden was deserted. It looked as if it had been neglected. Everything was so overgrown. There was a dried-up pond, a massive vegetable patch gone wild, a couple of fruit trees and a crumbling brick-built summer house with roses growing up the walls.

"Interesting!" said Lulu, deciding to start at the bottom of the garden where the dried-up pond was.

Primrose had said that solitary bees sometimes lived in the ground so Lulu peered into the pond's cracked clay bottom, but there were no bees there. She flew on, her eyes scanning the long grass, searching for holes. She was disappointed when she didn't find any, but maybe the vegetable patch had bees living in it. Lulu flew over a wigwam of bamboo canes with gangly runner beans growing up them, then, swooping low, she passed a thrush feasting on a bed of fat juicy strawberries.

The strawberries looked delicious, but there was no time for a picnic.

It was sad to see the garden so overgrown

and unloved when someone had clearly
spent a lot of time in it once.

"Concentrate!" Lulu told herself firmly.
There was no time to waste feeling sad –
she had to find the bees! Suddenly she had
a stroke of good luck. A slim bee with a
yellow-and-black striped back overtook
her. At once Lulu gave chase,

catching up with the bee at the summer house. The bee landed on the wall by the door, crawled along a rose stem then disappeared. Cautiously Lulu followed and noticed a small hole in the brickwork.

"So this is where you live," Lulu whispered. A shiver of excitement made her wings flutter.

Lulu examined the bricks and found more holes in the cement; some of the holes were empty, but lots were home to a single bee. The bees all seemed very content in their tiny hideouts.

Lulu felt like stamping a paw with frustration.

"None of these bees need my help!" she exclaimed.

She unrolled the sycamore leaf from round her wand and checked the map. She definitely had the right place, so what was going on?

"Maybe there are some other bees here," she said.

Lulu was about to set off again to look for more bees when she heard pounding

accompanied by heavy breathing. Startled and a tiny bit afraid, Lulu hid herself amongst the roses and cautiously peered out into the garden.

The pounding grew louder as Lulu saw a small girl with a very long rope coming down the garden path. She was trying to skip, but every few steps she tripped up.

The girl didn't get cross, but patiently untangled her feet before starting again. Lulu recognized her as the girl she'd seen in the magic mirror. She really needed help and while it would be fun to teach her to skip Lulu was in far too much of a hurry for that! With determined wing strokes she flew on.

Lulu wasn't sure what happened next. First there was a loud whooshing noise then something hit her hard, knocking her sideways. Lulu clutched at her wand as she tried to regain her balance. It was no good. Her heart raced as helplessly she plummeted through the air.

Chapter Three

Lulu was terrified she was going to crash to the ground and hurt herself. Tucking her head in, she hugged her knees to her chest, ready to break her fall with a roll. *Wumph!* Lulu landed on something soft. Slowly uncurling she stood up and looked around. Two bright blue eyes were staring at her. Lulu jumped and took a step back. Now she had a clearer view she realized she'd landed on the skipping girl's hand.

"Hello," whispered the girl, looking worried. "My name's Ruby. I'm sorry if I hurt you. I didn't mean to."

"It's OK. I'm fine," said Lulu, wiggling her wings to prove it.

"Good," breathed Ruby softly. "I'm practising for the sponsored skip tomorrow. It's to raise money for a new children's ward at the local hospital. It's not going very well though. I need some help, but we've only just moved here and Mum and Dad are too busy getting things straight to teach me to skip. But enough about me, who are you?"

A Lesson for Lulu

"I'm Lulu the Fairy Bear," said Lulu.

"What's a Fairy Bear?" Ruby asked.

"Fairy Bears are descended from the Great Bear, Ursa Major, and use magic to look after all the creatures and plants in the world. Today I've been given the task of helping some bees."

"Oh! Is there a hive nearby?" asked Ruby curiously.

"These bees all live alone," Lulu explained. "But I can't find them. The only bees here are the ones living in the walls of your summer house, but they look far too comfortable to need my help."

"There are bees living in the summer house?" Ruby gasped. "But the summer house is being knocked down the day after tomorrow. It's old and dangerous. I'm not allowed to go near it."

Lulu was so excited she jumped in

the air and turned three
somersaults.

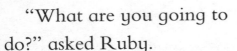

"Then those are
the bees who need
my help!" she
shouted. "Great.
Now I can get on
with my task."

"What are you going to
do?" asked Ruby.

Lulu stopped bouncing on Ruby's hand.

"Find somewhere else for the bees to live.
But I need to be quick about it or I'll miss
my chance to try out for the air-ball team
tomorrow. Air ball's my favourite sport."

"I might be able to help," said Ruby, her
face turning pink with excitement. "I've got
a book on wildlife. It's full of projects like
making bird feeders and bat boxes. There
might be something in it about bees."

A Lesson for Lulu

"Fantastic!" squeaked Lulu. "And when I've helped the bees, if there's enough time left, I'll teach you to skip."

"Thank you, Lulu," Ruby sighed happily. "That would be brilliant. If I get really good at skipping, I can raise lots of money for the children's ward. Wait here. I won't be long." With a smile as wide as a half moon Ruby rushed indoors to get her book.

While Ruby was gone Lulu practised throwing and catching with a tiny stone she'd plucked from the ground. She was concentrating so hard she didn't hear Ruby come back, and dropped the stone in surprise when Ruby ran down the path clutching a book.

"There are two whole pages, with pictures on bees," said Ruby, panting slightly. "It says here that you can make a bee hotel and there's a diagram to show

you how to do it. It's easy if you've got all
the right things and luckily we have."

She opened the book and pointed at
a picture of a bundle of pipe-like tubes
fastened together with twine.

"The pipes are lengths of bamboo cane,"
said Ruby. "There's a stack of them in the
vegetable patch.
They just need
cutting to the
right size
and tying

HELPING
WILDLIFE

PROJECTS RABBITS

BEES
BUTTER

together. When the hotel's finished we can hang it from one of the apple trees. It's not too far for the bees to move. They're going to love it," she added.

Lulu hovered over the book to examine the picture and then followed Ruby to the vegetable patch.

"Dad's hacksaw will easily cut through the canes only I'm not allowed to use it," said Ruby. "Tell me how many you need and I'll ask Dad to saw them when he gets home from work."

"That's all right," said Lulu. "I must complete the task by myself. If I fail, then I'll have to stay in Miss Alaska's class for another year when everyone else moves up to the seniors. Anyway, I *have* to finish the task today."

"Of course!" said Ruby, shaking her head. "Silly me! I forgot. You want to go

to the
air-ball try-
outs tomorrow. So
how will you cut the cane?"

Lulu grinned and waved her wand with
a flourish.

Ruby's blue eyes widened.

"Magic?" she asked in a whisper.

"Yes," said Lulu, examining the
bamboo canes. How long should she cut
them? She studied the picture in Ruby's

book then pointed her wand at the canes and chanted,

> "*Cut the canes, quick as a flash!*
> *Cut them quick, I need to dash!*"

When nothing happened Lulu stared at her wand expectantly then gave it a little shake.

"What's up?" asked Ruby. "Isn't it working?"

Lulu frowned. "It was fine this morning. Maybe I didn't say the spell loudly enough."

Clearing her throat she repeated the spell, clearly shouting the words. But once again the wand remained lifeless in her hand.

"Hmm," said Lulu, thoughtfully stroking the round topaz gemstone as it glittered in the sunlight. "Maybe the spell's not right. It did sound a little rushed."

She closed her eyes for a second then said slowly, "I'll try again."

Chapter Four

With a wide sweep of her wand Lulu aimed it at the bamboo canes and said in a loud, clear voice,

"Cut the canes, all of them, please,
To make new homes for the bees."

Lulu's wand glowed warmly and the handle began to shake. There was a series of loud popping noises, like mini explosions, and a jet of violet stars pelted from the wand's star-shaped tip. It was like a firework display; the stars whizzed high into the air then rained down on to the first bamboo cane and dissolved, cutting it to the right size.

Ruby's mouth opened in surprise.

"It's working," she squeaked. "You're so clever!"

Lulu felt bubbles of excitement rising inside her. She held her wand firmly, directing it at the other bamboo canes so the falling stars could cut them too. When the canes were the right size Lulu lowered her wand. Her wings were limp with exhaustion. Taking a deep breath she rallied herself and with a last burst of energy flew on to Ruby's hand.

"You don't mind, do you?" she asked as she sat down.

"Of course not!" said Ruby, beaming with delight. "That looked like it was hard work."

"It was," said
Lulu, flapping
her wings to cool
herself.
"Lucky I'm
so fit or
it would
have taken
much longer."

"Would you like me to finish making the
bee hotel?" Ruby asked.

"Thanks, but I'll be fine in a minute.
Tying the canes together is the easy bit."

When Lulu was rested she flew over to
a clump of sweet peas growing against
the fence and, settling on a bright purple
flower, had a long drink of nectar.

"Mmmm." Lulu wiped her mouth. "That
was delicious. Now I'm ready to carry on."

There was a coil of twine next to the bamboo canes. Lulu pointed her wand at it and began chanting,

"Tie the canes together as one;
Hang the hotel, in the shade not sun."

Lulu's wand trembled and the handle grew warm. A long stream of violet stars burst from the end and landed on the twine. At once the twine slithered towards the bamboo canes like a skinny snake.

"That's so cool," said Ruby.

The bamboo canes were moving now, rolling closer to each other until they'd formed a fat

bundle. The twine wound tightly round them then fastened itself in a knot.

Stars were still falling from Lulu's wand and she held the trembling handle steady, directing the stars over the newly made bee hotel. Slowly the hotel rose from the ground and floated towards a small apple tree at the edge of the vegetable garden.

"Faster," cried Lulu impatiently.

The bee hotel gathered speed. The loose ends of the twine snaked out and tied themselves to the tree's lowest branch with one end hanging slightly lower than the other.

"That was brilliant!" said Ruby, walking over to the apple tree to examine the bee hotel. "There's lots of room for the bees, but it's a bit wonky."

"That's OK," said Lulu, fluttering around the hotel to admire her work.

A Lesson for Lulu

"Your book says to tie the hotel at an angle to let rainwater drain from the pipes."

Ruby poured over her book. "It also suggests putting moss or small twigs between the canes to strengthen them," she said.

"I don't think I need bother with that," said Lulu. "The hotel seems very strong. Watch this." She did a series of back flips across the top. "See, it hardly wobbled!"

"Well, if you're sure . . ." Ruby was doubtful.

Lulu somersaulted in delight. "I'm very sure. I can't wait to tell Miss Alaska that I've finished my task already. But first let's give you a skipping lesson."

Diving to the ground Lulu picked up a spare piece of twine.

"Skipping is easy," she began. "Always

start with the rope behind you, like this.
Then swing it forward and jump, and
again, jump, jump, jump."

Lulu twirled her skipping rope faster and
faster.

"Once you've got the hang of it you can
do the fun stuff like double skip, cross over,

the twister, skip on one leg, change leg, go backwards." Lulu demonstrated, hopping so fast she became a blur.

"Stop!" begged Ruby. "I can't see you."

Panting slightly Lulu finally stopped.

"Sorry," she said. "I got carried away. It's your turn now."

Ruby picked up her own rope and, gripping the ends tightly, began to skip.

"Skip, skip . . . whoops!" called Lulu. "Untangle your feet and start again."

"It looks so easy when you do it," puffed Ruby unwinding the rope from around her feet. "So why can't I do it?"

"Are you concentrating?" asked Lulu. "You have to *really* focus on what you're doing. Here, watch me again."

But no matter how hard Ruby watched she didn't find the skipping any easier. Lulu tried to be patient, but she couldn't understand why Ruby was having such difficulty.

"I have to go now," said Lulu a short while later. "I want to get in one last air-ball practice before tomorrow. That's what you should do

too, Ruby, practise skipping. Oh, and it
might help if you tied your hair up so that
it's not flopping in your eyes."

Pushing her wavy brown hair out of
her eyes Ruby said passionately, "Thanks,
Lulu. This sponsored skip is really
important. The hospital desperately needs a
new children's ward."

Lulu fiddled with her wand. She felt
guilty about not being able to help Ruby
more. Impulsively she said, "Look, I'm not
promising anything, but if I can get away
after the air-ball try-outs I'll come back
and give you another lesson before the
sponsored skip starts."

Ruby's face lit up.

"That would be great! Thank you,
Lulu!" she cried. "And good luck with the
try-outs tomorrow."

"Thanks," said Lulu, thinking that luck

had nothing to do with her chances. If she got into the team, it would be through hard work and practice. Waving goodbye Lulu flew home.

Chapter Five

Lulu flew fast, neatly overtaking the insects that got in her way. As she reached Firefly Meadow she spotted Jet and a group of older Fairy Bears playing air ball near the stream. Lulu couldn't wait to share her success with Miss Alaska, but the lure of a game of air ball was too much for her and the practice would be useful. Altering her course she flew towards the players.

Jet was surprised to see her.

"Hi, Lulu, you've never finished your task already, have you?"

Fairy Bears

"I have," said Lulu, proudly puffing out her chest.

"Wow!" replied Jet. "You must have worked really fast. Have you come to play air ball with us now?"

A Lesson for Lulu

Lulu nodded and within seconds of joining the game she'd caught the ball.

"Lulu, here," called Hazel, a tall bear with bright blue wings.

Lulu passed to Hazel, then flew ahead of her, ready to catch the ball again. It was a fantastic game. Fired up with success from completing her task, Lulu played brilliantly. Afterwards several of the seniors congratulated her.

Flushed with excitement Lulu flew back inside the sycamore tree and into the Crystal Caves. She was still reliving the game when she fluttered into the class cave, where Miss Alaska was tidying up.

"There you are, Lulu," she said, as if she'd been expecting her for a while.

Lulu was too excited to notice Miss Alaska's look of disappointment.

"I finished my task," she gushed

47

confidently. "It was much easier than I thought. I had to make a new home for all the bees living in an old summer house because it's being pulled down soon. I built a bee hotel. The bees will be very comfortable there."

"Are you sure about that?" asked Miss Alaska.

Lulu was surprised how cross Miss Alaska sounded.

"Yes — it's a great hotel," she said defensively. "The bees are going to love it."

Clapping her yellow-and-pink wings together Miss Alaska fixed Lulu with a hard stare.

"Let me show you something," she said.

Bewildered, Lulu followed Miss Alaska over to the magic mirror. Whatever did her teacher want her to see? The tiny jewels studding the mirror's frame sparkled brightly as Lulu peered into the glass. There was nothing there. Not even her reflection. Suddenly a cloud of grey mist swirled across the mirror's surface. When it cleared Lulu saw a large untidy garden with a small apple tree by the vegetable patch.

"That's Ruby's garden!" she exclaimed.

The image in the mirror honed in on the apple tree. A bundle of sticks was hanging from the lowest branch. Lulu gasped and her wings turned ice cold as she suddenly realized it wasn't a bundle of sticks at all. It was her bee hotel. But whatever had happened to it? Half the bamboo canes had fallen out and were lying in the grass under the tree.

"You didn't do the job properly," said Miss Alaska crossly. "Your bee hotel is falling to pieces. Luckily none of the bees that had moved in were hurt. They

49

managed to fly away before their bamboo rooms collapsed."

Lulu was so shocked she couldn't speak. She could feel tears stinging her eyes.

"I'm sorry," she whispered at last. "I didn't mean to hurt anyone."

"I know," said Miss Alaska. "This time

you were lucky. But it's not good enough,
Lulu. You have to concentrate on the job
you're doing like you do when you're
playing air ball. You need to focus."

Lulu's wings drooped. She'd failed her
task. She'd let Miss Alaska and the bees
down and she only had herself to blame.

"Would you like another go?" asked
Miss Alaska softly.

Lulu stared at her teacher. Had she heard
her right? Was Miss Alaska offering her
another chance to take her task?

"You may retake your task tomorrow
morning, unless of course you'd rather take
part in the air-ball try-outs?" said Miss
Alaska.

Lulu's heart skipped a beat. On the one
paw she would be devastated to miss trying
out for the senior air-ball team. But on the
other paw she was thrilled to be given a

second chance to complete her task. She could try out for the air-ball team another time, but the bees needed Lulu's help now.

"Thanks, Miss Alaska. I'd like to take my task again tomorrow," said Lulu, her paws trembling.

Miss Alaska smiled.

"Well done, Lulu. You're making the right decision. Now remember: concentrate on what you're doing and don't try to rush the job."

"I will," said Lulu, nodding emphatically. This time she would focus on her task in the same way she focused on playing air ball.

That night, before climbing under her leaf duvet, Lulu set her alarm clock so she would wake up very early. Ruby had said the summer house was being pulled down the day after tomorrow, but what if the demolition company arrived sooner?

A Lesson for Lulu

Lulu was determined that her bees, as she now thought of them, would have somewhere to live before they lost their old home. The following morning Lulu jumped out of bed, groomed her pale gold fur and tiptoed to the kitchen so that she didn't wake Mum, Dad and big sister Flossy. After a hurried breakfast of honey cakes dipped in nectar juice Lulu went outside. The fresh morning air ruffled her fur and the sun warmed her violet wings as she soared across Firefly Meadow. Lulu hardly noticed. She was too wrapped up in her task. This time she wouldn't rush it. She'd take Ruby's advice and fill the gaps between the bamboo canes with moss to make the hotel strong and secure. As Lulu approached the garden she heard thudding. Was the summer house being knocked down already?

"Please don't say I'm too late!"

Fearful of what she might find in the garden Lulu dropped from the sky.

Chapter Six

As Lulu descended she could hardly bear to look. But to her great relief the thudding noise was just Ruby. Her hair was tied in two neat bunches and she had a determined look in her blue eyes as she practised skipping.

"Bother!" The rope coiled round Ruby's ankles, forcing her to stop.

Lulu landed softly on the tip of Ruby's freckled nose. Ruby giggled, going cross-eyed as she squinted to look at what was tickling her.

"Lulu!" she exclaimed in delight. "What are you doing here so early? How did the try-outs go?"

Lulu's wings went stiff with embarrassment as she explained that she hadn't completed her task properly and was missing the try-outs to put right her mistakes.

"That's awful!" exclaimed Ruby. "I'm so sorry, Lulu. I feel like it's my fault. I should have checked the bee hotel again before I went in, but I was so busy skipping that I didn't give it another thought."

"It's not your fault," said Lulu. "It was my task. I shouldn't have rushed it."

A Lesson for Lulu

"Would you like to borrow my book again?" asked Ruby.

"Yes, please," said Lulu. "And this time I'm going to check carefully what to do as I go along."

Throwing down her rope Ruby dashed inside to get her book. Meanwhile Lulu flew down the garden towards the bee hotel and was shocked to see the damage up close — it was a real mess. Lulu decided that the best way to fix the hotel was to take the whole thing down from the tree and then rebuild it. Lulu thought very carefully about a lowering spell before trying it out. She was pleased and relieved when the bee hotel untied itself and gracefully floated down to the grass. She flew closer and chanted a second spell:

> *"North, south, east, west,*
> *Make this hotel the very best."*

As Lulu spoke the words her wand grew warmer, then a bubbling stream of stars tumbled from the end and landed on the bamboo canes. This time when the canes rolled closer together and the twine began tying them up Lulu didn't hurry them. Instead she called out encouragingly, "You, move this way a bit. And you too, yes, you, the one sticking out from the others. Slowly now, don't rush."

She was so focused on her task she didn't hear Ruby approaching and jumped when her friend squatted beside her in the grass.

58

"I got it," Ruby panted, opening the book at the right page.

"Thanks," said Lulu. "Now let me see the bit where it says I need moss and sticks to fill the gaps."

With Ruby's help she set about gathering things. In no time at all there was a pile of material twice as high as Lulu for her to use to finish building the hotel.

"That should do it," she said, pushing a last clump of moss in between two bamboo canes to hold them firmly in place. Taking a step back Lulu admired her work. Then she checked Ruby's book once more.

"There's a list of helpful tips here. I missed that last time. It says that to make the hotel even stronger you can push the bamboo canes inside a plastic bottle that's had its ends cut off."

"We've got one!" said Ruby. "It's in the

recycling bin. I know because I rinsed it out and put it there. I'll go and get it."

Lulu couldn't bear to wait for Ruby to return so she went with her, flying alongside her shoulder. Lulu had to fly fast to keep up, which made her think that if Ruby could learn to use her rope properly she'd be brilliant at skipping. Once Ruby had retrieved the bottle it took a little bit of Fairy Bear magic to cut both ends off. Then Lulu let Ruby push the bamboo bee hotel inside it. She'd done the main part of the task by herself and as Ruby was so keen to help it seemed mean not to let her.

"That's going to be much stronger," said Ruby, holding up the bottle for Lulu to see.

Lulu thought so too, but this time she wasn't leaving anything to chance and crawled inside one of the bamboo canes to test it. She had to fold her wings behind her back because there wasn't much room. The pipe-shaped cane felt really solid, but cosy too.

"There's one thing left to do," said Lulu, crawling back out and hovering in the air.

Dramatically she waved her wand at the bee hotel.

"Hotel for the bees,
Go hang in the trees."

There was a flash of light and Ruby gasped as a long stream of violet stars arced from Lulu's wand and rained down over the bee hotel. Slowly the hotel rose into the air and flew over to the apple tree. The twine, sticking out from the ends of the cut bottle, snaked out and deftly tied themselves round the tree's lowest branch. The hotel rocked gently until it swung itself still.

"That was magic," whispered Ruby.

Lulu grinned. She loved it when her spells went right. Performing spells was similar to playing air ball. To be good at them required hard work and practice. Suddenly Lulu remembered the air-ball try-outs. It was still very early in the morning. If she hurried, she might make it back in time to compete. Ruby was thinking the same thing too.

"You've definitely passed your task this

time. The bee hotel looks even better than the one in my book. And if you're quick you might still make it back in time to try out for the air-ball team. It's this morning, isn't it?" Ruby twiddled one of her bunches.

"Yes," said Lulu, then remembering she'd told Ruby to tie her hair up she asked, "How's the skipping going?"

Ruby smiled. "It's easier now my hair doesn't keep getting in my eyes, but I'm still not very good. Luckily the sponsored skip isn't until this afternoon so I've still got time to practise."

"Practice makes perfect," agreed Lulu, repeating one of her grandmother's favourite sayings.

She dropped down on to Ruby's hand to say goodbye.

"Thanks for all your help. You made my task a lot more fun."

Fairy Bears

"It was fun for me too," said Ruby.
"Good luck with the air-ball try-outs."
"Good luck with the sponsored skip,"

said Lulu. "You're going to be brilliant. I just know it."

"Bye, Ruby," called Lulu, zooming into the air.

Lulu was buzzing with excitement as she flew back to Firefly Meadow. She'd done it! She really had completed her first task and if she flew fast she'd make it back in time for the air-ball try-outs too. Playing air ball for the school team, when she was still a junior, was Lulu's favourite daydream.

Lulu knew she needed to focus on air ball so that she could give her best performance, but she kept thinking about Ruby with her twinkling eyes and friendly smile. How was Ruby getting on with her skipping? Was she still getting tangled in the rope? Even though Ruby really needed to practise her skipping, every time Lulu had appeared she'd willingly dropped everything to help her build the bee hotel. An uncomfortable feeling began to swell in Lulu's tummy. The more she thought about it the more the feeling grew. Lulu had been selfish. She'd been too wrapped up with the air-ball try-outs to think about Ruby needing her help too.

Suddenly Lulu's ears began to twitch. She could hear cheering. Looking ahead she could see the edge of Firefly Meadow. A group of seniors was lining up on a branch of the sycamore tree, ready to begin the try-outs. Lulu flew faster, determined not to miss out on her chance of a lifetime. But halfway across Firefly Meadow the uncomfortable feeling inside Lulu grew so large it began to suffocate her. She slowed right down until she was hovering in the air like a dragonfly. Lulu had an important decision to make. Did she have the courage to make the right choice?

"Yes!" she exclaimed out loud.

Neatly turning a backwards somersault Lulu flew away. There was always next year for the air-ball try-outs, but Ruby needed her help right now.

Chapter Seven

When Lulu first arrived back at Ruby's
garden there was no sign of her friend. Had
Ruby got fed up and gone indoors? Would
Lulu be able to find a way inside to look
for her? Lulu's heartbeat quickened at the
thought of flying around Ruby's house on
her own. That would be tricky even for
sporty Lulu. She circled the garden once
more and to her relief found Ruby tucked
away behind a sprawling bush, skipping on
a paved area near a small round table with
two chairs. Ruby's face was bright red and

her cheeks puffed out
as she jumped up and
down.

"One, two, three,
four, five . . . Oh
bother!" Crossly
Ruby bent down
to untie the rope
that had somehow
tripped her up
again.

Eager to tell Ruby that
she'd returned to help her Lulu dived down
and landed on her hand.

"Lulu!" Ruby's face shone with delight
then suddenly it clouded. "What's up? Did
you forget something?"

"Yes. I forgot you. I'm sorry I rushed
away, but I'm back now to teach you
how to skip," said Lulu apologetically,

fluttering her violet wings.

"Lulu, no!" exclaimed Ruby. "That's really nice of you, but you mustn't stay to help me. There isn't time. You'll miss the air-ball try-outs if you don't hurry."

Lulu stood firm. "I'm not going to the air-ball try-outs. There'll be plenty of other chances to join the team. Air ball is just a game. What you're doing, raising money for the hospital, is different. It *can't* wait. I'm just sorry it took me so long to realize that. And I'm even sorrier that I wasn't a good skipping coach. I keep forgetting that sport isn't as easy for everyone as it is for me."

Tears sparkled in Ruby's blue eyes. "Oh, Lulu," she mumbled. "Thank you. You're the nicest friend ever."

Lulu didn't feel like she'd been a very good friend, but it was time to put that right. Purposefully she fluttered into the air. She was determined to teach Ruby how to skip.

"Put the rope over there," she instructed Ruby. "We'll practise jumping first. You need to jump high enough to clear the rope, but not so high that you'll hit your head on it. Rhythm is really important too."

Obediently, Ruby coiled up her rope and left it on the ground. Then standing with her feet slightly apart she began to jump.

"Good," called Lulu encouragingly. "Keep your feet together and bend your knees when you land."

Ruby was good at jumping and it wasn't

long before Lulu said, "Right, now let's try with the rope."

But jumping with the skipping rope was another matter. After Ruby kept getting her feet tangled Lulu called for her to stop.

"I think I know what the problem is," she said. "Your rope's too long. Try winding it round your hands a few more times."

Ruby wound the rope round her hands. Then, taking a deep breath, she began to skip again. But this time it was totally different. Her feet hit the ground together and neatly cleared the rope. On Ruby skipped, getting faster, her cheeks glowing red with exertion.

"Hooray!" cheered Lulu. "Keep skipping, Ruby."

Ruby skipped on until finally she stumbled.

A Lesson for Lulu

"Fifty-one," she panted. "Fifty-one skips! I've never even reached ten before. Thank you, Lulu! You're a brilliant teacher."

Lulu laughed. She'd really enjoyed helping Ruby and felt a glow of satisfaction at her friend's success.

"It's down to you now," she said. "Keep practising and there'll be no stopping you this afternoon."

There was one thing left that Lulu wanted to do. She flew to the vegetable patch to get the piece of twine she'd left there so that she and Ruby could skip together.

"Lulu, look," whispered Ruby. "Look at the bee hotel."

Lulu's wings flushed warm with pride as she hovered in the air near the bee hotel. Almost half the bamboo canes were already occupied by bees. Lulu somersaulted with delight.

A Lesson for Lulu

"Well done, Lulu. It's just a shame you missed the air-ball try-outs," said Ruby suddenly.

Lulu smiled. Things hadn't turned out quite as she'd planned, but seeing the bees safe in their new home and knowing that Ruby was going to raise lots of money for the hospital was a much better ending.

"It doesn't matter," she said. "Let's see if we can do one hundred skips before I go home."

With a lot of laughter Lulu and Ruby finally managed one hundred skips before collapsing in a heap on the ground. Lulu sat up first.

"I have to go now," she said, smiling at Ruby.

"Thank you for being such a brilliant friend," said Ruby.

"You too," said Lulu.

Impulsively she waved her wand in
a circle then, pointing it at Ruby, she
chanted,

> "*From me to you,*
> *A star that's true!*"

Ruby stared in amazement as a single violet
star popped from the end of Lulu's wand
and landed in her hand.

"It's a friendship star," said Lulu. "To
bring you good luck this afternoon."

"It's perfect!" said Ruby. "Thank you,
Lulu."

"Bye, Ruby." Lulu slowly rose into the
air.

"Bye, Lulu! Good luck with your next
task, and good luck playing air ball. I hope
you make the senior team one day."

Lulu pretended to shoot an imaginary

ball into a goal, then, with Ruby's cheers
ringing in her ears, she flew towards home.

As she reached Firefly Meadow Lulu
saw Mrs Pan standing on a branch in the
sycamore tree, holding a leaf. Sitting along
the branch was a large group of seniors.

Mrs Pan was calling out names.

". . . Hazel, Racer, Jet and last but not least Willow," said Mrs Pan, beaming at the Fairy Bears. "You've all made it on to the senior's air-ball team."

Lulu flew faster, determined to congratulate the seniors who'd been picked for the team.

"Well done," she panted, neatly landing next to Jet and Racer.

"Thanks," said Jet. "And bad luck for missing it. You'd have been a great addition to the team."

"There's always the reserves," said Racer kindly. "Mrs Pan is holding try-outs for them tomorrow."

"Lulu doesn't—" Jet started to say, but with a friendly smile Lulu cut him short. She'd learned so much over the last couple of days, but the thing she valued the most

was discovering the fun of doing things for others. Suddenly she wanted to be a reserve. She might not get to play very often, but at least she'd be helping the team – if she got picked of course!

"That's a brilliant idea," she said. "I'll definitely be trying out for the reserves."

Jet's face lit up. "Fantastic!" he shouted. "Then we'll come and cheer you on tomorrow, won't we, everyone?"

"You bet!" said Racer and Willow.

Lulu flew through the squirrel hole with Jet, Racer and Willow. There was so much to look forward to, starting with telling Miss Alaska she'd completed her task. Lulu was too excited to fly slowly.

"Race you to the Grand Door!" she called.

"You're on!" said Jet, Racer and Willow.

Lulu laughed and dived down the dark tree trunk, her wings a violet blur as her friends chased her home.

Fairy Bears Fact File

Lulu

1. Favourite colour – *violet*

2. Favourite gemstone – *violet topaz*

3. Best flower – *snapdragon*

4. Cutest animal – *fawn*

5. Birthday month – *November*

6. Yummiest food – *honey*

7. Favourite place – *Firefly Meadow and
the air-ball stadium*

8. Hobbies – *air ball, flying*

9. Best ever season – *autumn*

10. Worst thing – *cheats*

How to Build a Bee Hotel

Bees are very important. They help flowers and vegetables to grow.

Be a good friend to a bee and build them a home in your garden.

Things you will need

String or garden twine

Plastic drink bottle (washed)

Bamboo canes with hollow ends

Small twigs and/or some moss

Sharp scissors and an adult to do the cutting

How to make the bee hotel

1. Ask an adult to carefully cut the neck and the base off the plastic bottle.
2. Thread the string through the bottle leaving enough string to hang the bottle up.

3. Ask an adult to cut the bamboo canes to the same length as each other.
4. Tie the bamboo canes together tightly at each end, and then push them into the bottle.
5. Fill the gaps between the bamboo canes with the twigs or the moss (or both!).
6. Hang your bee hotel up in the garden making sure it is tilted down slightly to allow rain to drain out.

The best place to hang a bee hotel is on a shady, south-facing wall or tree – about 30 to 100 cm above the ground.

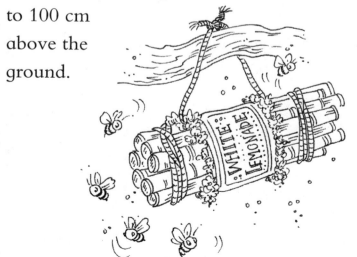